ANIMAL
RESCUE CENTER

The Unwanted Puppy

ANIMAL MAGIC

This series is for my riding friend Shelley,
who cares about all animals.

tiger tales

5 River Road, Suite 128, Wilton, CT 06897
Published in the United States 2016
Originally published in Great Britain 2006
by Little Tiger Press
Text copyright © 2006, 2016 Jenny Oldfield
Interior illustrations copyright © 2016 Artful Doodlers
Cover illustration copyright © 2016 Anna Chernyshova
Images courtesy of www.shutterstock.com
ISBN-13: 978-1-68010-028-0
ISBN-10:1-68010-028-9
Printed in China
STP/1800/0100/0216
10 9 8 7 6 5 4 3 2 1

For more insight and activities, visit us at www.tigertalesbooks.com

ANIMAL RESCUE CENTER

The Unwanted Puppy

by TINA NOLAN

tiger tales

ANIMAL MAGIC
RESCUE CENTER

 HOME

 ADOPT

 FRIEND:

MEET THE ANIMALS IN NEED OF A HOME!

SCOUT

Dumped in a
parking lot and
left to starve, Scout
is an adorable
cross-breed who
needs a home with
caring owners.

DOLLY

A 3-year-old
Labrador whose
owners left her
home alone and
never came back.
She is shy but
friendly and needs
a loving owner.

JEWEL

A long-haired
Persian with
beautiful eyes.
She needs friendly,
loving owners
who will let her
live indoors.

SITE SEARCH

NEWS

HELP US

CONTACT

$ DONATE!

COPPER and BAILEY

4-year-old Jack Russells who enjoy walks and would love to go to dog training classes. They would like to be adopted as a pair.

LADY

A 5-year-old border collie. She is clever, lively, and loads of fun and would love to learn new tricks from her new owner.

KITTENS

Two black-and-white, one tabby, and two brown. They are six weeks old, and looking for new homes in about two weeks' time.

Chapter One

"Come here, Copper! Bailey, lie down!"
Ella Harrison yelled at the two Jack
Russell puppies who were scampering
along the riverbank.

The puppies ignored her and ran on
through the long grass, wagging their
pointed tails. "Yip-yap! Yap-yap-yap!"

Ella groaned and dashed after them.
She grabbed Copper before he could stick
his head down a rabbit hole, and then
dragged Bailey out of the shallow water.

"Bad dogs!" she scolded.

Her brother, Caleb, stood on the bridge and grinned. "Bad dogs!" he mimicked. "Face it, Ella, you're lousy at this dog-training stuff!"

The Jack Russells wriggled and squirmed in her arms as she joined Caleb. She frowned at him. "Yeah, well, we're a rescue center, not a dog-training school. And anyway, if you're so good at it, where's Lady right this second?"

Lady was the Border collie he was supposed to be retraining. The dog

was hyper—always jumping up on people and running away. Her owner had dumped her at the Animal Magic Rescue Center, and it had been Caleb's idea to teach her good manners.

"Um...." Caleb looked along the riverbank. "I saw her a second ago. She was down there, playing with a stick."

"Oh! Isn't that her on the golf course?" Ella asked sweetly, pointing at a black-and-white collie charging across the smooth greens, jumping up at golfers, and then racing toward the rescue center.

"Uh-oh!" Caleb set off after the runaway while Ella giggled. She put her two puppies on leashes and followed more slowly, knowing that it was dinnertime and Lady would be heading for home.

But not before the young dog had bounded off the golf course onto the main street, raided a garbage can by the bus stop, and then rampaged through the Brookses' yard, next door to Animal Magic.

"Uh-oh!" Caleb said again, as he spotted Lady digging up their neighbor's lawn.

Ella held Bailey and Copper on tight leashes and ducked behind a bush.

"Shoo!" a high voice shouted. "Get away, you bad dog!"

"Oh, no, that's Annie's mom," Ella whispered to Copper and Bailey, who strained at their leashes, desperate to chase after Lady. "Mrs. Brooks is going to be in a major bad mood over this!"

Caleb dashed through the gate to catch Lady. "Heel, Lady!" he shouted, but to no effect. The collie stopped digging and ran off. She trampled through Mrs. Brooks's bed of bright red tulips.

"Uh-oh!" Ella reported the latest. "Now Lady has wrecked her flowers!"

Fed up with waiting, Bailey and Copper began to yap.

"Shhh!" Ella warned, while Caleb dived after Lady and chased her through Mrs. Brooks's roses.

Just then, as Ella waited with the terriers on the pavement outside the Brookses' yard, her dad drove up on his way home from work in his van. He leaned out of the window. "Trouble?" he asked.

Ella nodded, pushing her heavy hair back from her hot face. "Lady ran away!" she explained, struggling to hold the Jack Russells back.

"Come on, follow the van," Mark Harrison, Ella's dad, said quickly. "I'll park the van, then come back here to sort things out."

In a flash, Ella did as she was told. "See!" she said to Copper and Bailey, as her dad eased the van in through the gates of the rescue center. "That's what happens when you dig holes in lawns!"

Bailey wagged his tail. Copper wriggled between her legs.

"People don't like it!" Ella explained. "They so-o-o-o don't like it, do they, Dad?"

"So?" Heidi Harrison, Ella's mom, asked Caleb as they all sat down to dinner. "How did Linda react when you called to say you were sorry?"

"She went on about her flowers," Caleb mumbled with his mouth full. "She said I'll have to pay for new ones."

"Hmm." Mom was used to complaints from next door. Ever since she and Dad had set up Animal Magic, Linda and Jason Brooks hadn't had a good word to say about it. They thought it brought down the tone of the neighborhood. "Anyone would think Lady had committed a major crime, the way Linda's behaving!" she sighed.

"Yeah, Lady only dug a hole in her lawn!" Caleb sulked.

His dad shook his head. "Listen, this is one more thing for Linda to add to

her list. You know what she thinks of
Animal Magic—she'd love to have this
place closed down!"

The rescue center had only been open a
year. Mom was a vet, and it had been her
idea to rescue stray dogs and take in cats
and other pets that had been neglected.
She and Dad had found an old farm on
the outskirts of Crystal Park, and they'd
transformed it into a refuge for animals.

It had been a lot of work, but now they had a cat area and kennels, plus a third building to house other small animals like hamsters and rabbits. The old dairy had been turned into their mom's clinic where she microchipped, neutered, and vaccinated all new arrivals.

"They can't do that—can they?" Ella stared at her dad open-mouthed. "I mean, they can't close us down. What would happen to all the animals?"

"Don't worry, Ella," said her mom. "Linda Brooks is pretty much a lone voice. Most people in Crystal Park like what we're doing. You can tell that by our visitor numbers and the hits we get on the website."

"That's right," Caleb said, pushing away his empty plate. "Anyway, I'm off upstairs." He was still in a mood over having to apologize to Linda.

"'Thanks for a delicious meal, Mom!'" his dad reminded Caleb with a grin. "Are you working on the website?"

Caleb nodded and shuffled toward the stairs. "I'm setting up an Animal Magic forum, so people can email each other about how cool we are."

"Can I help?" Ella jumped up to follow.

"Nope," he muttered, disappearing up to his room.

So Ella shrugged and went to feed the animals instead, running across the yard to the cowshed that had been converted into kennels. She was greeted by a chorus of woofs and yaps.

"Hi, Bailey! Down, Copper!" she grinned, giving them their dishes of food and watching them gobble hungrily.

Each dog had a special diet for its size and age, arranged by Ella's mom. Ella went along the row, opening each kennel door and saying hello to runaway Lady, then to Dolly, a three-year-old Labrador whose owners had left her home alone and never came back. Next was Scout, the little black cross-breed who had been abandoned in a parking lot and left to starve. For each dog there was a sad story to tell.

"But with a happy ending!" Ella sighed, watching them eat. "You're here now!"

Dolly came up, asking to be petted. Scout joined her. Soon Ella was surrounded by happy, snuffling, tail-wagging dogs.

"We'll take care of you," she promised, giving them each a hug. "We'll find new owners and you'll live happily ever after!"

Chapter Two

"Can I see the kittens?" Annie Brooks asked.

It was early Saturday morning, and Ella had answered the door before anyone else was up. She dragged Annie into the house.

"Do you have any idea what time it is?" Ella demanded. Even though Annie was her best friend from school, she hadn't expected to see her this early.

Annie nodded. "I crept out before Mom and Dad were up."

"Is your mom still mad at us?"

Annie nodded. "I had to sneak out. I'm dying to see those kittens your dad found."

Ella smiled at her friend. She'd told Annie about her dad's latest rescue the day before, during recess at school. Her dad had found the kittens on Thursday night, in the parking lot behind the supermarket. "Come and help me give them some milk."

Quickly, the girls scooted across the yard, ignoring the yelps and barks from the kennels and heading for the adjoining cat area instead. They went in and closed the door. "Is anyone around?" Ella called.

A tall, sleepy-looking figure emerged from the small office.

"Hi, Joel." Ella smiled. "Have you

been here all night?"

Joel Allerton nodded. He was the main Animal Magic assistant, and that meant sometimes working nights. "I've got the weekend off, so I've been trying to get caught up with some paperwork before I leave. It's been quiet all night, thank goodness."

"Where are the new kittens?" Annie asked excitedly.

Joel took Ella and Annie to a quiet corner where the kittens were kept in a basket under a special heat lamp. Then he went off to prepare some warm milk.

Annie peered into the basket, which was lined with a red blanket and contained five adorable kittens—two black-and-white, one tabby, and two brown. They stared back with big, bright eyes, licking their lips with tiny, pink tongues and meowing hungrily.

"Oh!" Annie cried, carried away with delight. "They're adorable!"

Ella reached in and gently lifted the nearest kitten out of the basket. The helpless tabby nestled in her hand, licking her thumb with its rough tongue.

"Ohhh!" Annie cried, reaching out to take it. "So-o-o cute!"

Joel came back and showed her how to offer milk to the kitten from a small plastic dropper while Ella started feeding the rest.

"Here, little kitty!" Ella said, smiling as each hungry kitten opened its mouth and drank. "How could anyone put you in a box and dump you?" she wondered.

"Yes, how could they?" Annie echoed,

thrilled by the whole thing.

Ella fed four kittens and smiled as she watched them snuggle up in the basket to sleep. She grinned at Annie, who was still feeding the little tabby. "I can see I'll have to drag you away!" she said, lifting the sleepy kitten from her lap and placing it next to the rest.

"See you on Monday!" she called to Joel, whose eyelids were seriously drooping as Ella's mom came in to take over.

"There you are, Ella. And Annie, too. Ella, your dad wants you to walk the Jack Russells," her mom told her. "But have breakfast first."

"I'd better go, before Mom notices I'm gone," Annie decided.

She and Ella said good-bye in the yard, and then Ella wandered out of the front gate, along the street toward their house. She went in through a side gate, and was about to go back and walk the dogs when she happened to glance down and see a battered cardboard box placed carefully on one side of the road. The box was taped shut. It had air holes punched in the lid and one word scrawled in black marker.

Ella's heart missed a beat. She crouched down and read the name: "Honey."

Each time it happened, Ella felt sick. *How could you? So cruel! So unfair!* These were the thoughts that hammered at her head every single time someone dumped a pet at Animal Magic.

But then she clicked into action, pulling back the tape and opening the lid just a little bit. She peered inside.

A pair of dark brown eyes stared back at her.

"Don't be scared," Ella said softly. She could hear a tiny whimper and was able to make out a small cream shape. She pulled back the flaps and reached inside, lifting out a shivering, frightened *puppy*.

Ella's heart melted. "Oh!" she exclaimed, nestling the puppy against her. "You're beautiful! Shh, don't be scared!"

"What do you have there?" Caleb appeared. He'd been watching from his bedroom window and came to investigate.

Ella showed him the puppy. "Golden retriever," Caleb noted, reaching out to pet the puppy's head. "Probably about 12 weeks old." He didn't want to admit to his younger sister that he, too, wanted to cuddle and comfort the puppy.

He picked up the box and examined it for clues. "Have you looked to see if there's a collar?"

Ella checked around Honey's neck. "Nope. Is there an address on the box?"

"No, but I know where it came from." Caleb frowned as he read the print on the sides of the box.

Too busy with the latest arrival to
take much notice, Ella carried the
puppy toward the animal hospital.
Her mom came out to meet her, taking
Honey inside and immediately putting
her through the usual checks and tests.

"She's not microchipped," Mom
muttered, examining Honey under the
bright lights of the exam room. "And I
guess she's not vaccinated, either. She's
slightly dehydrated, but other than that
she seems okay. Ella, could you mix a
drop of glucose solution in this dish?
That's great, thanks. Look at her gulp
that down!"

Ella nodded. She'd begun to relax.
I wonder where she came from, she
thought. At least the owner cared
enough to dump her somewhere where

they knew she'd be taken care of. "I'll bet she's hungry," she said to her mom.

"Yes, I'm sure. Can you please get her some puppy food while I give her a shot?" Mom said. While Ella hurried off, her mom prepared a needle for the injection. "This might hurt a tiny bit," she told Honey, as if the puppy understood every word. "But it will stop you from getting any nasty bugs, and it'll be over soon."

Ella heard a high-pitched yelp. *Oh!* she thought, grabbing the food quickly.

Before long, the creamy bundle of fur had her nose deep in the dish and was happily chomping her breakfast.

"Good!" Ella's mom gave a satisfied nod.

"Totally cool!" Ella agreed. She was already looking forward to taking Honey to meet the other rescue dogs—

Lady, Dolly, Copper, Bailey, Scout, and the rest. Soon Honey would have a nice warm bed and friends to play with. Ella and Caleb would put Honey's picture and details on the Animal Magic website and they'd find a new owner for her. "You're so cute, you'll be snapped up in no time!" she whispered in the puppy's ear.

Honey gobbled greedily.

"Especially with those big brown eyes...."

Honey licked every last scrap from the dish.

"You're cuddly and soft.... In fact, you're totally adorable!"

Chapter Three

"Why do we have to go to see Grandpa?" Ella complained.

She sat next to Caleb in the cab of her dad's yellow van as they drove along the country lanes. She'd rather have been back at Animal Magic, playing with the kittens, walking the dogs, or feeding the small rescue animals such as Snowy, the beautiful white rabbit.

"Because!" Caleb said.

"But why?" she insisted.

Caleb sighed. "I showed you the box, didn't I? The one Honey was dumped in. You read the name on the side."

"So?" Ella didn't see the point of following up on any of the clues to Honey's owners that Caleb had found. "She's been dumped, remember? That means her owner doesn't want her."

"It said, 'Gro-well Garden Center,'" Caleb reminded her. "Grandpa uses these boxes to pack the plants he sells."

"Yeah, so?" Ella groaned. Caleb thought he was Mr. Super-Detective, but with him, two and two usually made five!

However, when she thought about it, this time Caleb was probably right. After all, the box was a possible clue, and their grandpa, Jimmy Harrison, did run Gro-well Garden Center.

"Plus, there's a date on the box, showing when it was delivered," Caleb insisted, pointing to the evidence that rested on his knees. "Grandpa can check it."

"So?"

"So maybe we can figure out who dumped Honey! Stop being totally clueless, Ella!"

"I know *that!* But why do we need to know?" Finding Honey's cruel owner was the last thing she wanted to do. "Why don't we just advertise on our website and find her someone nice and kind— someone who deserves to have her?"

"Hey, you two, give it a rest!" Dad sighed as he turned the van in through the wide gates of Gro-well Garden Center. "Your mom and I have decided it's worth trying to find out what

33

happened, so that's that."

He parked the van and they went to find Grandpa inside the huge greenhouse full of plants and flowers. They saw him at the cash register—a small man with combed-back gray hair, wearing a green vest over his neat checked shirt. Grandpa spotted them and waved.

Caleb, Ella, and Dad waited for a gap between customers, and then Caleb dashed up to the counter with the battered box. "Hi, Grandpa!"

"Hey, Caleb. What a nice surprise." Grandpa winked at Ella. "And how's my favorite granddaughter?"

"I'm your *only* granddaughter!" She grinned. Her grandpa was always winking and joking and making her laugh.

Caleb dove right in. "We need your help. Can you check the date on this box? It's one of yours, isn't it? Come on, Grandpa, this is urgent!"

"Whoa!" Grandpa pleaded as Caleb ducked under the counter. "Slow down. Do you want to knock me clean off my feet?"

"He's playing detective," Ella warned. She explained her brother's idea about tracking down Honey's owner. "Don't ask me why!" she added with a shrug.

"Another case for Inspector Harrison!" Grandpa joked. But he was willing to help with any information he could, asking Dad to assist his customers while he and Caleb checked the computer records.

Caleb clicked the mouse, flashing through recent deliveries and sales. He soon found what he was looking for. "The date on this box is last Monday. And here's a list of sales you made that day."

"Totally amazing, Caleb!" Ella muttered. "Grandpa probably had hundreds of customers on Monday. It could be anyone."

But Grandpa was examining the box more closely. "No, it's bigger than the ones I usually use," he said thoughtfully.

"I would pack shrubs in this rather than flowers. And there was one customer here on Monday who bought a dozen laurel bushes for a hedge she's planting at the front of her house. I made a note of her name and address, in case she wanted me to deliver any more."

"Who was it, Grandpa?" Caleb jumped in.

"Let's see." He checked a notebook by the side of the cash register. "I remember now—I used three identical boxes for the laurels, just like this one. Yes, here it is—her name is Mrs. R. Penny, 16 Oak Grove, Lakewood!"

"I think *you* should keep her!" Annie exclaimed.

It was Saturday afternoon, and she and Ella were playing with Honey in the yard at Animal Magic.

"I wish!" Ella sighed. There were only two strict rules at the rescue center that her mom and dad never broke. One was that no healthy animal was ever put to sleep. The other was that Ella and Caleb were not allowed to keep any of the rescue pets.

"Otherwise, within a week our house would be overflowing with every furry creature that crossed our doorstep!" Dad had pointed out when Animal Magic had first opened its doors.

It was a hard rule, especially when Ella fell for a puppy like Honey.

"But she's so-o-o cute!" Annie lay on a bench, letting Honey crawl all over her.

The furry puppy pushed her nose under
Annie's shirt collar, slipped sideways,
and was quickly caught by Ella.

"Why don't *you* give her a home?" Ella
asked.

Annie sat up and pulled her hair
out of Honey's reach. "Are you joking?
My mom would never let a dog in the
house—not in a million years!"

Ella nodded. "Yeah, how could I forget?" The Brookses thought pets of any kind were noisy and messy. That was partly why they hated having Animal Magic next door. Yet the idea of finding Honey a new home nearby was definitely tempting. "You couldn't kind of ... um ... work on your mom, could you? You know, convince her that she'd soon grow to love Honey if she gave her a chance?"

Annie shook her head. She took the puppy from Ella and cuddled her tightly. "You don't know how strict my mom can be!"

Just then Linda Brooks came out into her yard and from behind the tall bush her high voice called Annie's name.

"Oops, better go!" Annie said, giving the puppy back to Ella. "Mom doesn't know where I am, and you know she doesn't like me hanging out with you at Animal Magic."

"See you later!" Ella called as her friend sped away.

"Number 16 Oak Grove, Lakewood!" Caleb had made a note on the palm of his hand in pen. He was in the clinic, showing his mom the evidence they'd gathered.

"Nice work," Mom told him. She was busy combing through a gray cat's tangled coat. Jewel the long-haired Persian had been found injured and filthy in a vacant lot in town.

Caleb sat on the edge of the table and swung his legs. "Tell Ella that," he mumbled. "She's making up all kinds of excuses to keep us from finding Honey's owner."

Mom looked up, a slight frown line between her clear gray eyes. "Don't tell me—she's fallen in love again!"

Caleb nodded. "I've been trying to tell her that there might have been some mistake—maybe this Mrs. Penny didn't want to get rid of the puppy, or maybe she did but now she's changed her mind and is really sorry...."

"There's no need to tell me," his mom interrupted, petting Jewel before she placed her back in her basket. She went to the window and looked out into the yard, where Ella was playing with Honey. "It's Ella you need to convince."

"Or not!" Caleb said, abruptly jumping down and heading for the kennels. The door opened to a chorus of yelps and barks. "What do I care if Ella's gone crazy over the puppy. What else is new?"

Mom shook her head and sighed.

Caleb grabbed a leash, opened Lady's kennel door, and strode back into the clinic. "Tell her, will you, Mom? See if you can get through to her!"

"Tell her what?" his mom asked, still gazing thoughtfully out the window.

Caleb headed out into the yard, looking grown-up and serious. "That Dad and I are going to drive to

Lakewood tomorrow morning to find
Mrs. Penny, whether Ella likes it or
not!"

Chapter Four

"I don't care what Caleb says," Ella told Honey early the next morning. She crept close and pointed a camera at the golden-haired puppy. "I'm taking your picture and putting you on our cool new website!" She and Caleb really wanted the website to work. Whenever a rescue animal arrived at Animal Magic, the first thing they did was take a picture and upload it to the site.

Honey cocked her head to one side

and stared at the camera. She blinked at the flash.

"Sweet!" Ella grinned, popping Honey into her kennel, and then dashing back to the house. She raced upstairs to Caleb's room where he sat at his computer. "Quick—we have to upload this photo!" she exclaimed.

Caleb clicked on the Animal Magic homepage. "Working Our Magic to Match the Perfect Pet with the Perfect Owner!" it said. "Who's the picture of?" he muttered.

"Honey!" Ella replied. "And it's so-o-o cute!"

"Hm." Caleb clicked his mouse to bring up the new forum page, where a new message had appeared recommending the center. "I can't put her on yet. We still have to check out her history, remember?"

"Yes, but!" Ella ignored her grumpy brother and hooked up the cable to upload the image. Whatever he said about trying to find the puppy's owner, she was dead set on getting Honey's details up there as soon as possible.

"Ella," said Caleb, "Honey might not need a new home—not if we link her back up with Mrs. Penny and everything works out okay."

"Yeah, but Sunday's a good day for people to log on and find a new pet!" Ella protested. "What's wrong with getting started today?"

She turned to her dad, who had just come into the room. "Dad, Caleb's being bossy!"

Dad took a long look at his lively, brown-eyed daughter. He guessed

what was on her mind and he knew
she wouldn't want to hear what he was
about to say. "I called Mrs. Penny and
didn't get an answer," he told her quietly.
"But I still think it's worth a drive into
town to see what's been going on."

Ella frowned. "Mrs. Penny doesn't want
Honey!" she protested.

"Maybe. But Dad, tell Ella we have to
check it out just in case," Caleb objected.

He could think of half a dozen reasons why Honey had ended up at Animal Magic.

Their dad nodded. "Come on," he said with a sigh. "Let's get this over with!"

"Don't forget to stop off at Mrs. Armstrong's house to pick up her cat!" Mom reminded them as they climbed into the delivery van that Dad used for work. So far there hadn't been enough money to buy a special van for Animal Magic, so they had to make do. Mom stooped to pick up an envelope from the mat.

Ella sat with Honey curled up on her lap. "Don't worry. We won't make you

go back to Mrs. Penny if you don't want
to," she whispered.

The puppy made herself comfy.

"Ready?" Dad asked.

"Let's go!" Caleb said, map in hand.
"Oak Grove is on this side of Lakewood,
since we go in on Cabot Drive."

"I know where it is," his dad said. "It's
in a nice part of town."

Mom closed the door and studied the
white envelope. It had been delivered
by hand, addressed to Animal Magic
Rescue Center.

She opened it and glanced down at
the signature. It was signed by their
next-door neighbors.

Uh-oh!

50 Main Street
Crystal Park

Dear Mr. and Mrs. Harrison,

We wish to inform you that we have begun an official
campaign to have your rescue center closed down.
As you know, local residents feel strongly that the noise
from the kennels and the ever-growing number of animals
housed in the sanctuary pose a threat to the quiet, rural
nature of the town.
We are presently talking with town planners and other
interested parties, as well as collecting a list of signatures
from residents.
Of course, we are sorry to cause bad feeling between
neighbors, but considering the circumstances, we feel it
cannot be avoided.

Yours sincerely,
Linda and Jason Brooks

Mom's hand shook as she read the
letter. "No way!" she exclaimed. "This
place is our life. The animals need us.
I will not let them close us down!"

"Okay, we have to turn left here," Caleb told his dad, looking up from his map at the rows of houses. "James Street leads to Cabot Drive."

Instead, Dad drove straight. "I promised your mom I'd visit Mrs. Armstrong and pick up her cat," he reminded Caleb and Ella. "She lives just down here."

Feeling tense, Ella petted Honey and stared out the window. "Why doesn't Mrs. Armstrong want her cat?" she asked, as they pulled up outside a small fenced house with neat lace curtains.

"Oh, she wants to keep Patience, but the retirement home that she's moving into doesn't allow cats," her dad explained.

Ella nodded. "What a shame," she said. She saw the curtains twitch, then a few moments later, the front door opened and a frail elderly lady appeared.

"I'll wait here with Honey," Caleb said as Ella and her dad climbed out of the van.

"Patience is ready for you!" Mrs. Armstrong said, putting on a brave face, although her eyes looked red. "We've said our good-byes!"

Inside the dim house, Ella saw a sturdy pet travel carrier, and inside it a sleek orange cat with a white face and one white paw. As her dad picked up the carrier, Patience let out a loud meow.

The sound brought fresh tears to

Mrs. Armstrong's eyes.

"Don't worry. We'll take good care of her," Dad promised. "We're not called Animal Magic for nothing!"

"And we'll find her a wonderful new home," Ella added.

Mrs. Armstrong dabbed at her cheeks. "I know you will," she said softly. She followed them to the door and watched them step out into the sunshine with her beloved pet. "Good-bye, Patience!"

The cat meowed as Dad lifted her into the back of the van and quickly drove off.

"That was so sad!" Ella sighed, taking Honey back onto her lap. The puppy wriggled and strained to see the cat in the back of the van. "This is so not a good day!"

Ella stared out the window again as her dad pulled into the traffic. Soon the streets grew wider, with the houses set further back from the road. They passed a park with a duck pond and came to some even grander houses behind high stone walls.

"Oak Grove!" Caleb announced.

"Number 10 ... number 12 ... 14...,"
Dad slowed the van and pulled up
outside the wide gates of number 16.

Honey began to whine and struggled
to see out the window.

"She recognizes the house!" Ella
gasped. "I think she's scared!"

"Ella, calm down," her dad said. He
looked at the closed iron gates and
curved driveway leading between tall
trees to a porch with stone pillars and a
stained-glass door.

But Ella didn't listen. "I'll bet Mrs.
Penny is a dragon-lady!" she cried. "I'll

bet she was cruel to Honey and scolded her and smacked her if she made a mess in her posh house! That's why she kicked her out and dumped her on our doorstep. And that's why Honey is shaking now!"

Even Caleb seemed to have second thoughts. "What do you think, Dad?" he asked quietly.

Dad paused. He tapped the steering wheel and clicked his tongue. "We go ahead and do what we planned," he decided at last. "You two wait here with Honey."

"Please don't let anyone be home!" Ella breathed.

Crunch-crunch-crunch! Dad trod quickly up the gravel driveway. He rang the bell and waited for the door to open.

Chapter Five

Dad rang once, twice, three times.
There was no reply.

Ella and Caleb watched from the van.

After a while a short, stocky figure
appeared around the side of the house.
The man marched right up to Dad and
stood with his arms folded, his legs wide
apart.

"Who's he?" Ella muttered. "He
doesn't look very friendly."

"Dunno. Might be Mr. Penny." Caleb

shrugged. "I wish we could hear what they were saying."

They waited impatiently for their dad to come back.

At last he came back down the driveway and climbed into the van. "That was Mrs. Penny's tenant," he told them. "Not a very friendly type—he didn't even give me a chance to explain why we were here. But he says Mrs. Penny had gone away for the weekend. They should be back later today."

Ella breathed a sigh of relief. At least she wouldn't have to part with Honey just yet. She hugged the puppy closer to her.

"What do we do now?" Caleb asked.

"Nothing we *can* do for now," his dad replied, turning the van and heading for home. "I guess we take Honey back to Animal Magic."

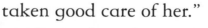

Ella's first job when they got home was to carry Patience into the cat unit and have her admitted.

Ella's mom examined the orange cat and nodded. "She's in great condition," she told Ella. "Well fed, with a nice glossy coat. Mrs. Armstrong has taken good care of her."

Ella took a photo. "We can put her on the website right away. We'll say she'd be perfect for a family with young children—I think she'd like that!"

Her mom nodded. "No luck with finding Honey's owner, I hear?"

Ella shook her head and quickly changed the subject. "Caleb says that two people want to come and see Copper and Bailey later today. And someone from town called to say she likes the look of Jewel from her photo on the website."

"That's good," Mom said, as if she had something on her mind. "Ella, find your dad and ask him to come here, would you, please? Maybe you and Caleb can get your own lunch."

Ella set off with the message but forgot to deliver it when she spied Annie through a gap in the bushes. "Hi, Annie! Do you want to take Honey for a walk?"

Annie was around there in a flash, dressed in a new pink top and bright white sneakers.

Ella looked down at her own faded shirt and muddy boots. "How come you're always so neat?" she grinned.

Annie batted her eyelids. "Blame my super-neat mom!" she groaned. "Come on. Where's Honey's leash?"

Setting off with Honey and Lady, Annie and Ella headed for the river, where Annie got her sneakers all dirty, and Lady went swimming.

"Go on, you try, too!" Ella urged Honey. "It's fun!"

The golden retriever crouched on the smooth white pebbles, reaching out one tiny paw to test the water.

"Oh!" Annie cried.

"Swim!" Ella encouraged.

Boldly, Honey waded into the shallow

water. But it was cold, and she soon turned and scampered back.

"Wimp!" Ella laughed, watching Annie pick up the dripping puppy. Then she spotted Lady, swimming strongly toward the far bank. Which meant only one thing! The runaway was up to her old tricks.

"Lady, come here!" Ella called.

Lady reached the bank and shook herself. She cocked her head toward Ella, decided to ignore her, and looked toward the golf course.

"Uh-oh! Lady is going to get us into trouble again!" Ella groaned. What should she do? Run to the bridge or wade in after Lady? She decided to plunge in, gasping as the cold water reached her knees and then her thighs.

But soon she reached the far bank and
threw herself at the surprised collie.

"Gotcha!" she cried, quickly putting
her on the leash.

She turned to Annie and Honey. "Take
the bridge!" she shouted. "I'll meet you
on Main Street."

"No need to wait!" Annie said,
putting Honey on the leash and
heading downstream. "Go home and
dry off. I'll see you later!"

"Heel!" Ella told Lady over and over.

They'd skirted around the golf course and made it to Main Street, but now Lady was pulling at the leash, eager to reach home.

Suddenly, she heard a bicycle behind her, and Caleb and his best friend, George, pulled up alongside her.

"What happened to you?" Caleb asked, spotting her soggy jeans and boots.

"Hey, Caleb, I'll see you later," George said, pedaling on.

"Don't ask!" she muttered at Caleb. "Oh, I have a picture of Patience for us to upload. Plus, we'd better get moving with the website profile for Honey, after what we found out this morning."

"Maybe," Caleb shrugged.

"What do you mean, 'maybe'? The Pennys don't care about Honey. They dumped her because they had no one to take care of her when they went away!"

For once Caleb didn't argue. "I've got to go and see what George wants," he mumbled, as his friend reappeared waving frantically. "Just don't do anything until I get back, okay?"

"Okay." In any case, Ella was cold and wet. So without waiting for Annie and Honey, she decided to head for home.

When she got there, she was surprised to see that the front yard was full of cars. Joel's Beetle was there, even though it was his weekend off. And among the group of people standing outside the clinic door, Ella recognized

Pete Knight and Debbie Fielding, two of the volunteers who helped out at the center. "What's up?" she asked Joel, as Lady pulled her toward the kennels.

"We've been told not to say anything. You'd better ask your mom," Joel answered with a worried look.

"Heel, Lady!" Ella pleaded. She went inside to find her mom and dad deep in conversation. "What's up?" she said again.

"Nothing," Dad said quickly, obviously covering something up.

Mom sighed and shook her head. "Ella and Caleb will find out soon enough," she argued. "It's going to be all over town before the end of the day."

Ella swallowed hard. "What is?" she asked quietly, sensing that she was about to hear something very bad.

Her mom held out a letter. "It's the Brooks," she explained. "You know how they don't like having Animal Magic next door to them?"

Ella nodded. She crouched and put her arm around Lady's neck.

"The bad news is, they've started a campaign," Mom said. "It's official. Linda and Jason Brooks want to get Animal Magic closed down!"

Chapter Six

"They can't close us down. We're a charity!" Joel said firmly, as Ella walked into the yard with her mom and dad. "We don't run Animal Magic to make money. We do it for the love of animals!"

"Of course they can't," Debbie agreed. "We've been here for more than a year now, and the Brookses are the only people in Crystal Park who are against us!"

Ella listened anxiously. Whatever the grown-ups said, she couldn't help picturing what it would be like if the Brookses won. What would happen to Scout and Patience, and the dozens of other unwanted pets who needed new homes? What would happen to Lady? She looked down at the mischievous collie who nuzzled close, demanding to be petted. What would happen to little Honey?

Come to think of it, where was Honey?

Ella glanced across the yard, and then walked to the front gate to look down Main Street. How come it was taking Annie so long to walk back?

Puzzled, Ella was about to turn and go back when Caleb came charging toward her on his bike. "George has heard a rumor. He's just given me some really bad news!" he cried, screeching to a stop.

"Yeah, I know," Ella said hurriedly. "Caleb, did you see Annie by any chance?"

"They want to close Animal Magic!" he cried, ignoring her question. He leaped off his bike, threw it against the fence, and dashed inside.

Handing Lady to Joel and leaving Caleb to find out the details, Ella walked up Main Street. In the Brookses' front yard, Mr. Brooks was mowing the lawn. Mrs. Brooks was clipping her rose bushes.

She saw Ella and stared.

Ella felt Mrs. Brooks' stare bore into her. She hurried on, expecting to see Annie and Honey coming toward her any second now.

But she got all the way to the old footbridge across the river without finding them. Now she began to panic, looking this way and that, checking that they weren't on the golf course or along the riverbank. "They can't just vanish!" Ella muttered, wondering uneasily what Mrs. Brooks would say if she found out that her daughter was missing with one of Animal Magic's rescue dogs. Maybe Annie had had an accident. Or maybe Honey had run away!

She was just about to dash back home for help when she saw a small movement in the long grass growing in the shade of the stone bridge. Then she heard a sharp, high yelp.

"Honey?" Ella called, climbing carefully over some rocks.

"*Yip-yip!*" came the reply.

"Annie, are you there? It's me—Ella!" She stumbled, but eventually reached the long grass. Under the shadow of the bridge she found her friend.

Annie sat cross-legged, holding Honey in her lap. Her cheeks were streaked with tears.

Ella sat beside her. "What's wrong? Why didn't you come home?"

For a long time Annie didn't answer. "It's Honey!" she said at last.

"Is something wrong? Is she hurt?" Ella asked anxiously.

Annie shook her head and cried. "I adore her! I don't want her to go. That's why I didn't bring her back!"

It was Ella's turn to be silent, as she watched Honey snuggle up to Annie in the peaceful shade.

"Do you understand?" Annie asked.

"Yeah," Ella said softly. "Of course I do. It happens to me every time we take in a stray or a pet that someone doesn't want anymore. I always want to keep every animal we rescue!" She eyed Annie warily. "I've just heard about your mom and dad planning to close us down."

"Oh, no! I had a feeling that they were going to do it!" Annie said miserably. "They're always talking about it."

"Well, now they're really going to go ahead and do it," Ella said, realizing how hard it must be for her friend.

"This is awful. I'm never going back!" Annie shook her head in disbelief.

"You have to," Ella argued. "But Annie, it doesn't make any difference— I'll still be your friend."

Annie looked up uncertainly. "Sure?"

"Absolutely!" Ella insisted. "I mean, honest! We're friends, Annie—no matter what your mom and dad do!"

"You busy?" Caleb asked Ella that evening. He wandered into her room, hands in pockets, trying to look casual.

A single thought had run through her head all evening. *Animal Magic has to stay open!* "Leave me alone. I'm tired!" she groaned.

"Listen, Ella—about Honey. I've been thinking."

"La-la-la-la!" She blocked her ears.

"What if Mrs. Penny isn't to blame? I mean, she could've given the box away after she was finished with it. Or maybe...."

"La-la!" Ella sang. But he was getting through to her all the same.

Caleb frowned. "Okay, don't listen to the facts. Go right ahead and jump to conclusions!" He went out and banged the door.

Ella sat on her bed deep in thought. Okay, so Caleb bossed her around, like all big brothers did. But maybe he was right this time and she was letting her feelings about Honey get in the way. There was a mystery behind this, and one that needed to be solved.

But Ella would never admit that to Caleb. No way!

Instead, she sat cross-legged on her bed and came up with a plan.

Chapter Seven

The next day at school, Ella let Annie in on part of her secret. "After school today I'm going somewhere special," she told her. "I can't tell you where exactly!"

Annie's green eyes sparkled. "That's not fair. Tell me!"

"Not until after I've done it." Ella stood firm. "But if it works out, it'll mean that the Honey mystery is solved!"

The mention of Honey's name sent

Annie off into a daydream. "If ... if only my mom would let me have a dog!" she sighed.

"I know," Ella replied. "I'd love to keep Honey!" Then she shook her head. "Anyway, the point is, you don't need to wait for me after school."

"Huh?" Annie broke out of her dream world.

"Don't wait for me when school is over!" Ella hissed across the aisle.

She tingled with excitement at the thought of what she planned to do, but she wouldn't say anything more.

At the front of the room, Mr. Carpenter looked up from his desk. "Ella Harrison, stop gossiping and get back to work!" he warned.

The morning and then the afternoon dragged by. Ella's nerves were on edge and she couldn't concentrate—all she could think about was her plan. It seemed like forever, but at last the school day ended. Children poured out of the classrooms into the playground, hurrying to catch their buses. But Ella hung back.

"Get going, Ella, or you'll miss your bus," her math teacher, Miss Jennings, told her.

"It's okay. I'm not riding the bus today," Ella replied, pulling Caleb's city map out of her bag and slipping out the side door.

Once on Cannon Street, she headed quickly uphill toward the old manor, a major landmark towering over the houses and shops. From there, she looked down busy Cabot Drive, checked the map, and walked on.

Ten more minutes and she'd be there. Five more minutes …. Ella began to recognize the streets that her dad had driven through the day before. She saw the park with the duck pond and the big houses behind high stone walls.

"Oak Grove!" she said quietly,

stuffing the map back into her school
bag. She noticed the new bushes planted
on either side of the front gate. "Mrs.
Penny, here I come!"

The loud ringing of the doorbell made
Ella jump as she stood on the steps in her
school uniform, waiting for someone to
come to the door. Her stomach churned,
and her throat felt dry.

She planned what she would say: *Why did
you dump your puppy?* And if Mrs. Penny's
answer was good enough, Ella would go
on with: *I know where she is. Do you want her
back?* This was her grand plan, but now that
it came down to it, she wasn't sure that it
was going to work.

When no one came to answer the

door, Ella peered through the stained-glass panel into the empty hallway. The whole house seemed still and quiet.

She was about to give up when the angry man from yesterday came stomping around the side of the house, like he had done before. "What do you want?" he demanded.

Ella gasped. The tenant's eyes were small and mean. He acted like he owned the place. "Is Mrs. Penny here?" she asked in a small voice.

Ignoring the question, the tenant came closer. "Don't I know you?" he asked. He'd obviously seen her sitting in the van with Caleb. "Didn't you come here yesterday in the yellow van?"

She took a deep breath and nodded. "My dad came to ask Mrs. Penny if she'd lost her puppy."

The man blinked. "What puppy?" he
asked. "The Pennys don't own a puppy."

"A golden retriever, about 12 weeks
old," Ella insisted, though her legs were
shaking. Why was this man so angry
and scary?

He shook his head. "Nah, you've
made a mistake."

"Can I just check?" Ella was about
to ring the bell one last time when the
tenant barged between her and the door.

"Didn't you hear me? You've got the wrong house. Scram!"

"Hey!" Stumbling back down the steps, Ella was forced to give in. She turned and ran down the driveway and into the street.

What now? She stood on the pavement and caught her breath. She couldn't believe how the man had acted. She didn't like how he'd talked, and no way should he have stepped in front of her like that.

"You okay?" a voice asked.

Ella spun around on the pavement to see Caleb standing there.

"Don't ask!" he grinned. "I knew you were up to something—I could tell by the look you've had on your face all day. Then I saw you sneaking out the side door after school."

"So you followed me?"

Caleb nodded. "I have to take care of my little sister," he said, "especially when she's cooked up some crazy, half-baked plan!"

Chapter Eight

"I don't believe a word that tenant said!" Caleb said when Ella told him what had happened.

"Me neither," she agreed. "But what can we do?"

"Nothing right now. It's a shame that Mrs. Penny didn't come to the door." As usual, Caleb stayed cool. He waited for Ella to calm down after her encounter with Mrs. Penny's tenant.

"I don't think she's home, but we could

wait here until she gets back," Ella suggested, glancing up and down Oak Grove.

"Yeah, and what do we tell Mom and Dad?" Caleb pointed out. "That we went behind their backs to find Mrs. Penny and got thrown out by the tenant?"

Ella sighed. "Yeah, you're right—it doesn't sound good."

"No, we have to catch the next bus home. Mom and Dad have a lot on their minds without us causing more trouble."

Reluctantly, Ella and Caleb set off down the broad, tree-lined street. They brushed past low-hanging branches of pink blossom, stopped to let a car drive into its driveway, and then headed on toward Cabot Drive.

"We can get the number 32 bus back home on the corner," Caleb was saying.

But Ella was only half-listening. She'd spotted a woman and a fair-haired boy talking to an elderly man with a walking stick on the other side of the road. The woman was pointing to a piece of paper taped to a lamppost. The man shook his head. The woman took the little boy's hand and walked on.

"Wait!" Ella called to the woman, hurrying across the road without Caleb.

"Ella, come back! We're going to miss the bus!" he yelled after her.

But she had a strong gut feeling about that piece of paper on the lamppost. She reached it and began to read.

"Ella!" Caleb shouted, jogging after her. He stoppped next to her, and his jaw dropped. "Honey!" he gasped.

The paper showed a photo of a cute, golden-haired puppy, and above its head was the word "lost" in large letters.

LOST

Honey. 3 months old.
Much loved family pet.
Please call 555-9754
or contact Ruth Penny,
16 Oak Grove, Lakewood

"Come on!" Ella cried, skirting around the elderly man with the stick. She raced around the corner to Cabot Drive. "Hey!" she yelled when she saw the woman and the little boy. "Wait!"

"Honey, it's me, Scott!"
Ruth Penny's son picked
up his puppy and
hugged her tightly. He
and his mom were in
the kennels at Animal
Magic. "Do you
recognize me?"

Honey licked his hands
and cuddled close. She yipped and
yapped and wriggled with joy.

"Oh, Honey, I thought I'd never see
you ever again!" Scott whispered as
he buried his face in the puppy's soft
golden fur.

His mom stood beside Ella's mom
and dad, smiling and sniffling at the
same time. "I couldn't believe it when
Ella ran up to us," she said. "We were

putting fliers everywhere to try and find
Honey, but without Ella and Caleb, we
wouldn't have stood a chance!"

"So what exactly happened?" Mom
wanted to know. "Who dumped Honey
on our doorstep?"

"Tony Ellans." Mrs. Penny began to
explain.

Mom gave a puzzled frown.

But Ella was buzzing with excitement.
She jumped right in. "The tenant!"
she cried. "It turns out he hates dogs
because they bark and they can be
vicious and he says they're a pest. I
mean, he really hates them!"

Dad nodded. "Like Linda next door,"
he muttered.

"So he waited for Mrs. Penny and
Scott to go away for the weekend to see

Scott's dad."

"My husband's working in Virginia right now," Ruth Penny explained. "I asked Tony to take care of Honey for us. It was the first time I'd risked leaving her."

"And no one knew he had this thing about dogs, because he kept quiet about it," Ella continued. "Anyway, he saw his chance on Saturday morning. He found a box in Mrs. Penny's shed, stuffed Honey into it, and drove out to Crystal Park, where he knew no one would recognize her. And that's how she ended up with us!"

"Thank goodness!" Mrs. Penny's smile shined through her tears. "You've all taken such good care of Honey for us!"

"That's our job," Mom said quietly.

"For as long as we're able to do it."

"What do you mean?" Mrs. Penny asked.

Ella's mom went on to tell Ruth about the fight they had on their hands for Animal Magic to stay open.

"Let me help!" Ruth said. "I'll get people in Lakewood to sign letters of support. I'll tell all my friends what a great job you do!"

"Cool!" Caleb said, sticking his head around the door and shoving Annie into the room. "See!" he told her. "I told you we'd find Honey's owners!"

Annie sidled in and stood next to Ella.

"I take it you'll be looking for a new tenant now?" Dad asked Ruth.

She nodded. "I've decided not to report Tony to the ASPCA, but I've already asked him to move. Next time we'll find someone who likes pets!"

"So everything's back to normal." Mom glanced at Ella and Annie. "It's time to say good-bye."

Scott Penny handed his puppy to Ella. "Say thank you, Honey!" he told her.

Honey nuzzled Ella's cheek. She was as soft, silky, and adorable as ever. It was hard to let her go. But Ella handed the puppy to Annie. "Now you," she sighed.

Annie cuddled Honey. "Good-bye!" she whispered.

Scott's blue eyes shone as he took Honey back. The beautiful puppy wriggled and wagged her tail. Good-bye!

"And now?" Caleb asked, holding the

door open for Scott and his mom and watching them walk across the yard.

In the background, dogs yapped and cats meowed.

Mom, Dad, Ella, Caleb, and Annie stood shoulder to shoulder under the painted sign that read "Animal Magic."

"Now we get on with our job," Mom decided.

"We match the perfect pet with the perfect owner!" Caleb said.

Ella grinned and added, "And we don't let anything get in our way!"